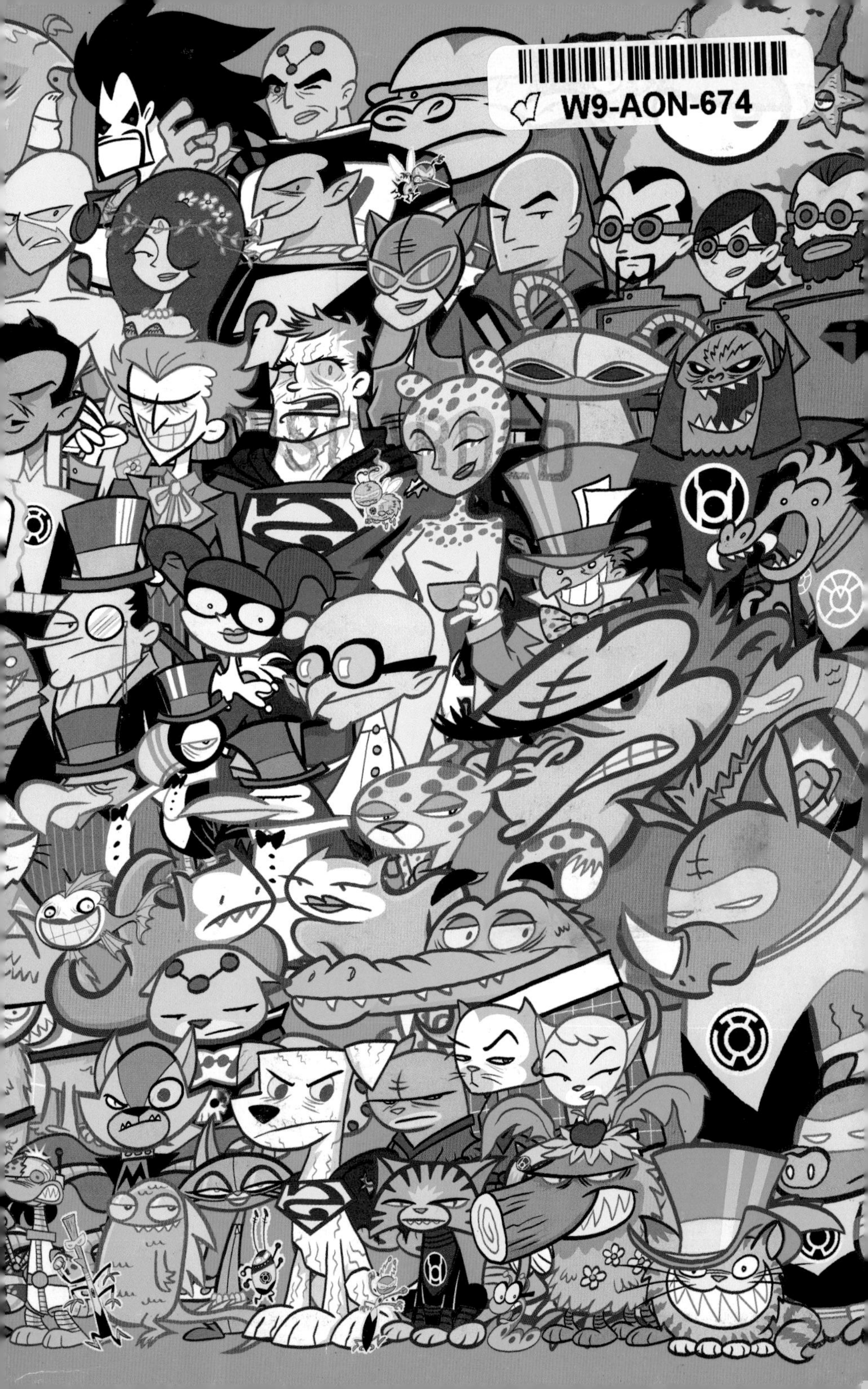

DC™

SUPER-PETS!

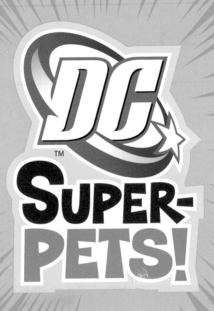

by Donald Lemke

The AMAZING
Mini-Mutts

illustrated by
Art Baltazar

Superman created by
Jerry Siegel and Joe Shuster

Batman created by Bob Kane

Picture Window Books™
a capstone imprint

Starring...

THE AMAZING MINI-MUTTS!

BRAINICAT!

SPRIGHTLY STEVE!

LUNA MOON!

ACE
THE BAT-HOUND!

KRYPTO
THE SUPER-DOG
AND THE
SPACE CANINE PATROL AGENTS!

REX
THE WONDER DOG!

FENDOR & SEN-TAG
THE GREEN LANTERNS!

TABLE OF CONTENTS!

SUPER-PET HERO FILE 012B :
THE AMAZING MINI-MUTTS

SPRIGHTLY STEVE

Giant
Heart

Super-
speed

Small
Size

LUNA MOON

Ultra-
snout

Giant
Heart

Small
Size

Super Hero Owner:
CLOEY

Species: Canine

Place of Birth: Earth

Age: One (human year)

Favorite Food:
Itty-bitty Bones

Bio: After being pawpicked by Krypto, these prep-school pups completed Bowwow Boot Camp and became the world's newest Super-Pets!

4

Super-Pet Enemy File 012B:
BRAINICAT

Wicked Smart

Super-strength

Cold-hearted

Super-villain Owner:
BRAINIAC

BOWWOW BOOT CAMP

"Welcome to Bowwow Boot Camp!"

said **Krypto.** The Super-Dog stood

outside a secret school located on an

icy mountain. Many of the World's

Greatest Pooches had trained at this

exact spot. Today, the newest class of

canine cadets had finally arrived.

Krypto stared at the fluffy faces in front of him. "Be proud," he said to the prep-school puppies. "The five of you are the picks of the litter!"

"Yes, but remember . . ." a deep voice interrupted. The class turned and spotted **Ace the Bat-Hound.**

Batman's Dog Detective walked up and down the lineup of pups. He gave them all a sniff with his snout. **"In the end,"** said Ace, **"only one of you will be named Top Dog."** SNIFF

A few brave bowwows wagged their tails excitedly. Others shook with fear.

Krypto placed his paws around a couple of quivering canines named **Luna Moon** and **Sprightly Steve.**

"Ace is right, but there's no need to worry, you two," said the Super-Dog. "We'll teach everyone a few old tricks."

Krypto pointed to a nearby training course. On the frozen field stood more hairy heroes, including **Rex the Wonder Dog,** the **Green Lanterns Fendor** and **Sen-Tag,** and all of the **Space Canine Patrol Agents.** Each waited near an obstacle that would test the might of the mutts.

"Now, come on," Krypto exclaimed. "It's time for your first *pup* quiz!"

With a burst of power, the Super-Dog flew toward the training course. Behind him, the pack of pups let out a whimper. Then they quickly followed their lightning-fast leader into the air.

Before they could catch him, one of the pups perked up his ears.

RUMMMBBLE! "Did you hear that? Did you? Did you?" asked Pound Paulie, an excited golden retriever.

The other pups stopped and listened.

 "Look!" shouted Luna Moon. She pointed a trembling paw toward the mountain top. A giant rock had broken loose from the icy peak. It tumbled toward the training course. **"What should we do?"** she asked.

"Run!" said her pooch pal, Sprightly Steve. He tucked his tail between his legs and quickly scooted away.

"Pound! Pound!" suggested Paulie instead. The dopey retriever darted toward the ball-shaped boulder.

Pound Paulie smashed through the rock with his thick skull. The remains rained down like spilled kibble.

"Nice work! You passed the first test," said Krypto. The canine cadets landed next to him on the course. "Strength is important for a Super-Pet!"

Luna Moon and Sprightly Steve hung their snouts. The puny pooches weren't strong like the others.

Just then, the ground shook.

Luna, Steve, and the other canine cadets spun on their hind legs. Behind them stood a giant snow monster! The blizzard beast licked its icy teeth and stomped its frozen feet. **WHOMP!**

This time, a pup named Pyro the Poodle stepped up. The fire-breathing pup opened her mouth. She blasted the beast with a hurricane of heat.

In an instant, the poodle melted the snow monster into a puddle.

Nearby, the Green Lanterns smiled. The creature had been their creation and another test for the canine cadets.

"Good job!" said Krypto, patting the poodle's frizzy fur. "Many great Super-Pets have super-breath! Now, who's ready for the next challenge?"

RUFF! RUFF! RUFF! Four of the pups barked with excitement.

Krypto looked around. "Where are Luna Moon and Sprightly Steve?" he asked the others. The pups pointed toward a shivering snowbank.

With his X-ray vision, Krypto spotted the missing mutts. **FWOOSH!** The Super-Dog blasted apart the pile of powder in one breath.

"What's wrong, you two?" Krypto asked Luna and Steve.

The pocket-sized pooches looked up at the Super-Dog with sad puppy eyes. **"I'm not super-strong,"** Luna Moon finally said. **"Yeah,"** agreed Sprightly Steve, **"and I don't have super-breath."**

"We're just two puny pooches!" they said together.

"Follow me," Krypto said with a smile. "I need to show you something."

The Super-Dog led them toward the edge of the training course. There, towering above the snow, stood rows and rows of dog statues. "Do you know who these canines are?" asked Krypto, pointing up at the marble mutts.

Luna and Steve shook their heads.

"These are the most powerful pooches ever!" said Krypto. The Super-Dog walked up to the first statue and wiped snow from its name tag.

"This is my father, **Zypto,**" said the Super-Dog. "A strange serum gave him wings to fly." Krypto moved to the next statue, which was larger than all the rest. "This is my grandfather, **Nypto.** An alien's ray made him a giant!"

The Super-Dog moved to one final statue and wiped its name tag clean. "And this is my great-grandfather, **Vypto.** Do you know how many powers he had?" asked Krypto, turning toward Luna and Steve.

They shook their heads again.

"None!" Krypto exclaimed.

Luna and Steve gasped.

"It's true. My great-grandfather didn't have any powers," explained the Super-Dog, "but he was the smartest of us all!"

Krypto stared down at the canine cadets. "You see, every pooch has a special skill," he said. "Now, let's head back and discover your own!"

Luna and Steve began wagging their tails. They grinned from ear to ear. But then, just as quickly, a sudden shadow covered their fluffy faces in darkness.

The Super-Dog glanced over his shoulder and into the sky. This time, **_he was the one who looked worried._**

Chapter 2

ATTACK OF BRAINICAT

Back on the training course, the Super-Pets and their canine cadets stared into the sky as well. A flying saucer floated above them. It now completely blocked out the sun.

"Ooh! Another test!" shouted a pup named Husky the Hurler. "I'll take it!"

While the others cheered, the husky

dug up giant chunks of earth with his

powerful paws. He hurled them at the

alien spacecraft with all his might.

SMASH! The chunks of rock

and ice shattered against the flying

saucer. They didn't even make a dent!

"Stop!" Krypto cried out. He landed back on the training course with Luna Moon and Sprightly Steve. "This isn't a doggy drill. It's the real deal!"

"For once, he's right!" yelled a voice from above. A green-haired cat appeared on the edge of the saucer. "Those puny pebbles can't hurt me!"

"Brainicat!" shouted Krypto, spotting his alien enemy.

"Skip the introductions," said the cosmic cat. "You pea-brained pups are all the same."

Ace the Bat-Hound returned with a growl. "Then you haven't met this mutt," he barked. "No one forgets me!"

BANG! Ace fired a Batarang and wire at the feline's flying saucer. The super-strong hook bounced off the spacecraft like a tennis ball.

"Your bark is worse than your bite, Bat-Hound," shouted Brainicat. "But if you wanted a closer look at my spacecraft, you simply had to ask."

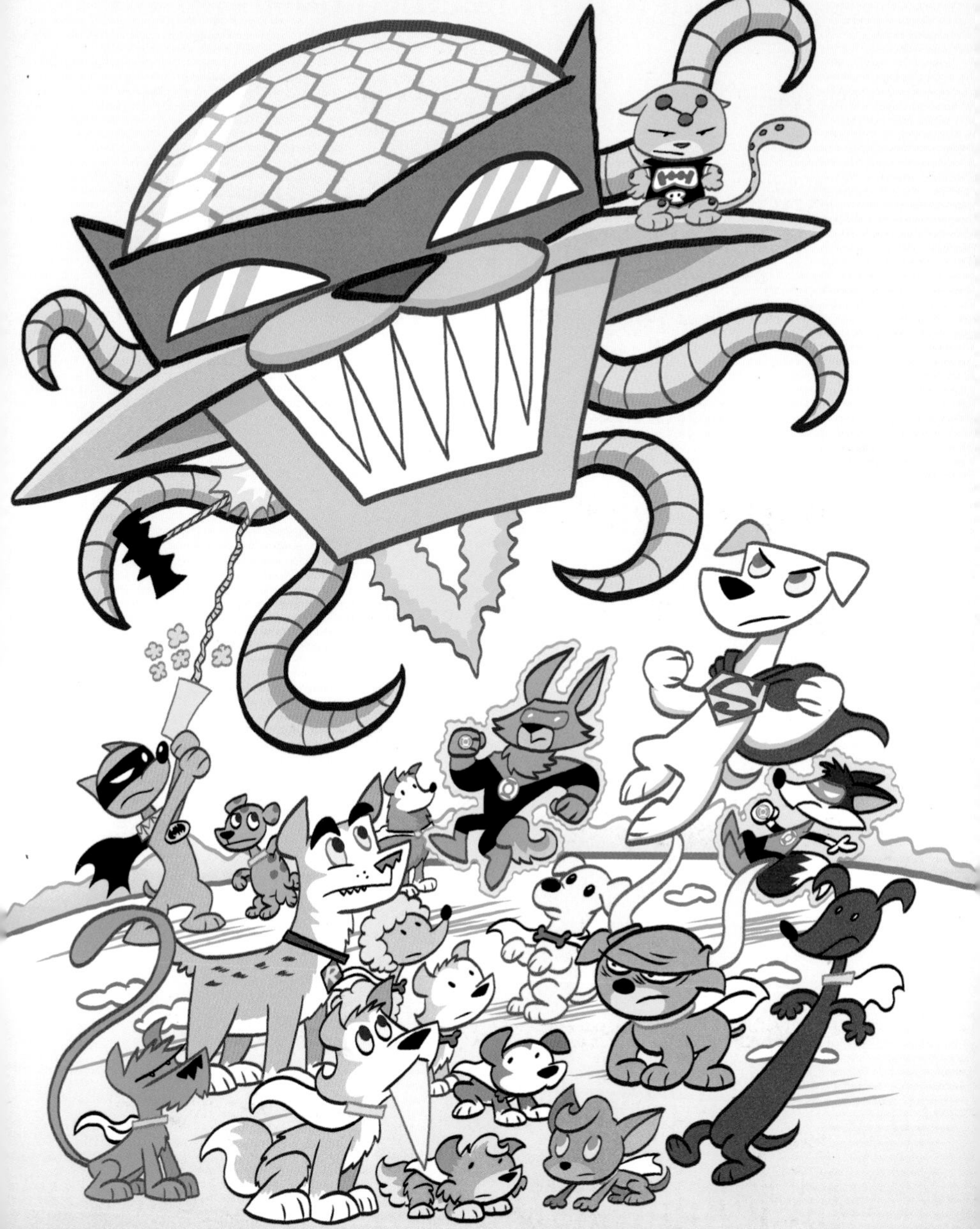

A sudden light beamed down on the Super-Pets and their class. The ground shook like the back of a wet dog.

"I'm going to be sick!" said Husky the Hurler, trying not to toss his cookies.

Then, in the blink of a cat's eye, everything stopped.

"What happened?" asked Ace.

"I'm not sure," Krypto replied, "but it smells like trouble."

Luna Moon raised her schnoz and gave a quick sniff. "Look!" she shouted.

Above them, the flying saucer had
disappeared. In its place floated the
head of Brainicat! His evil grin stretched
across the sky like a storm cloud.

"Enjoying your new doghouse?" his
voice thundered down from above.

The canine cadets were confused. But like his master, the Bat-Hound had unmatched detective skills. He used them to study his surroundings. **"We're trapped!"** Ace finally said.

"What do you mean?" asked Krypto.

"Please, let me explain, Bat-Hound," said Brainicat. "Or should I call you Rat-Hound? After all, you're now smaller than a mouse!"

To the Super-Pets, the cat's evil plan suddenly became clear. Clear as . . .

"Glass!" the Super-Dog exclaimed.

FWOOOOSH!

Krypto flew into the air. Instead of soaring through the clouds, he smacked into a ceiling of thick glass.

BONNK!

"Foolish pooch!" shouted Brainicat. "You'll never escape from that bottle!"

"Bottle?" Krypto wondered aloud.

"A milk bottle," added Brainicat, licking his gigantic chompers, "from this morning's breakfast, of course."

"That explains the smell," said Ace.

"Joke all you want, Rat-Hound," purred the cosmic cat. "My collection of canines is finally complete!"

The Super-Pets and the canine class moved toward the wall of the bottle. They pressed their fluffy faces against the glass. Dozens of other bottles filled the inside of Brainicat's spaceship.

Each bottle contained many miniature mutts. RUFF! RUFF! They barked for help.

"Using my incredible shrinking ray, I've kenneled canines from around the galaxy!" explained Brainicat. "Now, it's time to return to my home planet, where I'll rule you all! HAHAHAHA!"

Brainicat screwed a metal lid with tiny air holes onto the top of the milk bottle. Then he let out a long yawn. "If you'll excuse me, I'm going to take a catnap during the ride," he said. "We'll land back on Colu in fourteen years."

The canine cadets gasped.

"Don't worry," added the evil cat. "That's only one hundred dog years!"

CHAPTER 3

DOGGY DUO!

RUFF! RUFF! The prep-school puppies barked with anger. They chased their tails and ran in circles. They didn't know what to do!

"I'll break us out of here with my power ring!" shouted Sen-Tag, the Green Lantern. Fendor agreed.

"The Space Canines are at your service as well, Krypto," added one of the patrol agents.

"Thanks, everyone!" said the Super-Dog. **"But maybe the cadets should crack this case — I mean, bottle."**

Ace couldn't believe his ears! **"Are you sure about this plan?"** the Bat-Hound asked his superpowered pal.

"Real danger isn't planned, Ace," replied Krypto. "But a Super Pooch — a Top Dog — is always prepared."

WOOF! The canine cadets started barking excitedly. The up-and-coming pups couldn't wait to step up!

Pyro the Poodle and Husky the Hurler took the challenge first. The fire-breathing dog blasted the bottle with hot air. The heroic husky scraped the glass with his powerful paws.

"Whew!" they both said after a mighty effort. But the super-strong glass was too tough to melt or crack.

"Pound! Pound!" Paulie was ready to give it go as well.

FWOOOOOSH!

The eager retriever soared toward

the top of the bottle. He smashed the

metal lid with his thick skull. **BONK!**

It was screwed on too tight. The dopey

dog fell to the ground with lumps on

his noggin.

"Way to use your head!" joked Husky the Hurler. "Those bumps are almost bigger than Luna and Steve."

The other cadets let out a laugh.

Luna and Steve were too busy to care. They studied the bottle top high above. The lumps on Paulie's head perfectly matched the air holes in the lid. If Husky was right, they could easily squeeze through them.

"**Krypto, I think we've discovered our special skill!**" said Luna Moon. She pointed at the milk bottle's top.

The Super-Dog glanced up. Then he gave the miniature mutts a knowing look. "I thought you would," he said.

FWOOOOOSH!

Without another word, the puny pups soared into the sky. Their teeny-tiny capes flapped behind them like pieces of loose thread.

Within seconds, they reached the top of the milk bottle.

As small as fleas, Luna Moon and Sprightly Steve flew through the itty-bitty air holes. Then they landed on the floor of the spacecraft and scoped out their surroundings.

 "Now what?" Sprightly Steve asked his puny partner.

 "There!" shouted Luna Moon. She pointed toward a high-tech control panel on the wall. It was covered with dozens of red, glowing buttons. Each button had a number, just like each milk bottle.

"Those must reverse Brainicat's shrinking ray!" said Steve.

Luna raised her snout. "Something smells like sour milk," she said.

Steve spun around. "More like a sour *puss*!" shouted the mini mutt, pointing into the air. "That doggone cat is back!"

Brainicat towered above them, showing his sharp claws.

"What made you puny pups think you could escape?" he meowed.

Luna and Steve looked at each other and then back at the cat.

Sprightly Steve raised a proud paw. "Every dog has its day!" he shouted.

FWOOOOSH! The quick canine rocketed into the air. He buzzed Brainicat's head like a bee. The cosmic cat swatted wildly at the mini mutt.

"Go, Luna! Go!" Sprightly Steve yelled to his beagle buddy.

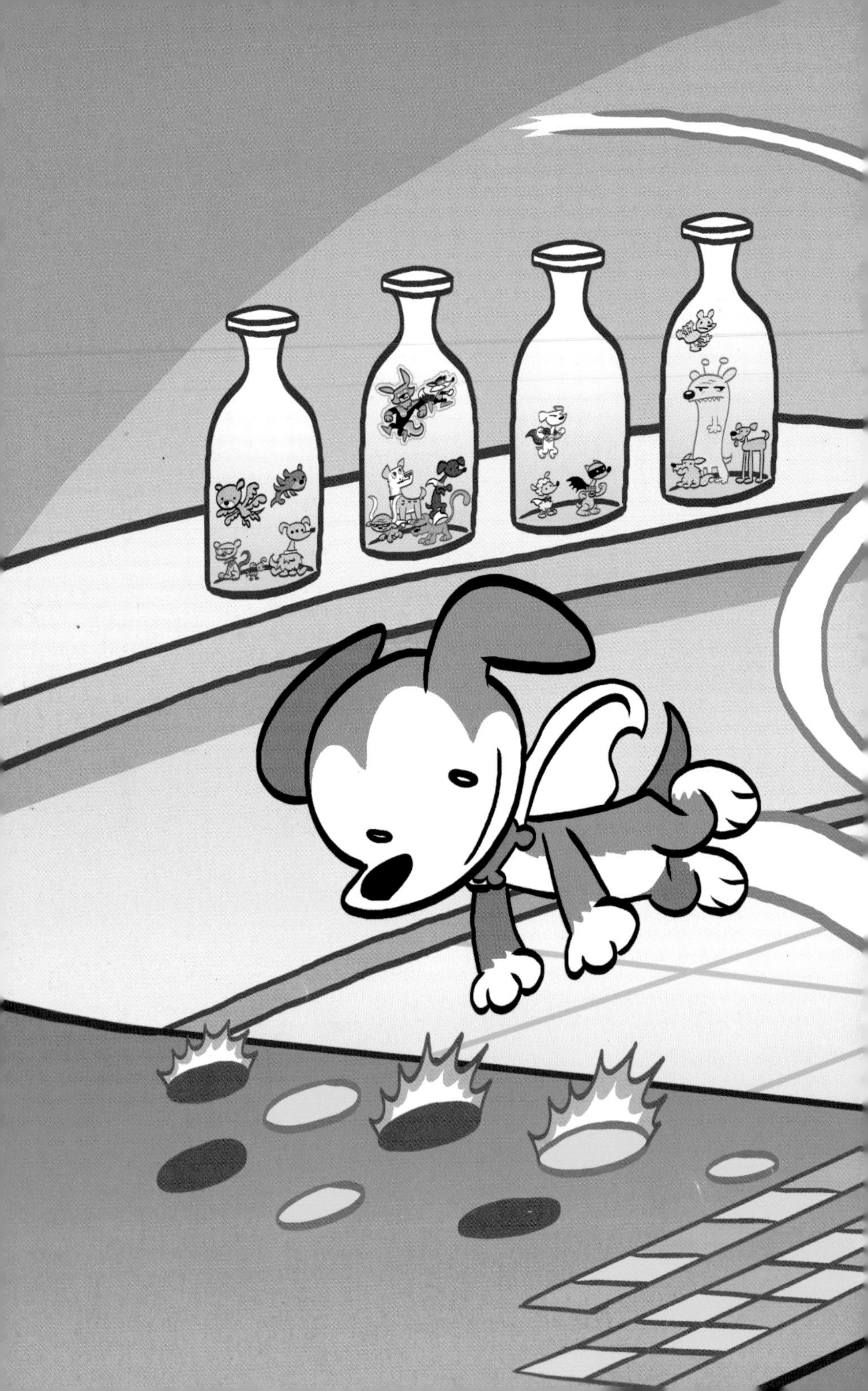

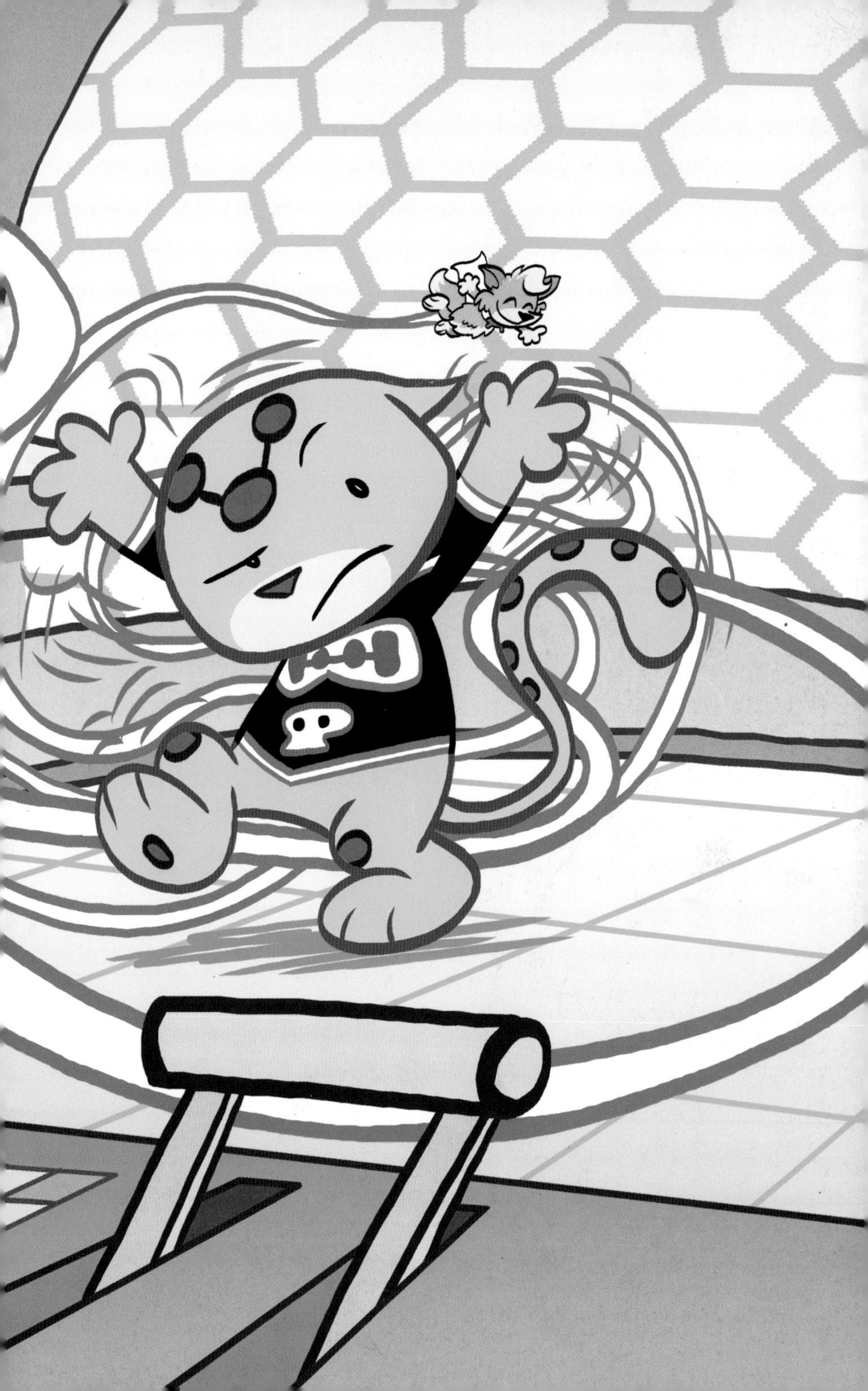

Luna Moon sped toward the control panel and started pushing the red buttons. Nearby, the bottled bowwows cheered! One by one, they disappeared back to their home planets, where they returned to normal size.

Finally, a single milk bottle remained. It contained the Super-Pets and the canine class. Luna Moon held her paw toward the final button.

"Looks like your dog days are over," said a voice from behind. Brainicat was back!

"That button will save your friends," said the cosmic cat. "But you two will remain mini mutts . . . FOREVER!"

Sprightly Steve landed on the control panel next to Luna Moon. "What's so bad about being bitty?!" he shouted.

Then, together, the two puny pooches pressed the final button. BEEP! In an instant, the Bowwow Boot Camp and the Super-Pets blasted back to Earth.

"Nooooo!" screamed Brainicat. The furious feline leaped at the mini mutts, but they were too teeny to trap.

SMAAAASH! He landed
face-first on the control panel and sent
the spaceship into hyperdrive!

"Time to find the doggy door!" said
Sprightly Steve. Luna leaped on her
puny partner's back.

They flew out of the spacecraft through an itty-bitty air vent. As Brainicat's ship tumbled into space, the mini mutts soared back to Earth.

WHOOSH!

At Bowwow Boot Camp, the Super-Pets and the canine class waited near the statues of the World's Greatest Pooches. They greeted their hairy heroes with wild applause.

Sprightly Steve landed next to them. "No need to thank us," he said.

 **"We were just doing our duty,"** added Luna, hopping off his back.

"Exactly!" Krypto exclaimed.

The Super-Dog scooped up the puny pups. They were no bigger than the pads on his paw. "Your actions today have made us all proud," he said, glancing at the statues behind him. "That's why, for the first time ever, we're naming *two* Top Dogs!"

Krypto held Luna Moon and Sprightly Steve into the air.

"Class, meet the world's newest Super-Pets," he said with a smile. **"The Amazing Mini-Mutts!"**

Everyone cheered with glee, but Luna and Steve had the biggest smiles of all.

END!

KNOW YOUR HERO PETS!

1. Krypto
2. Streaky
3. Beppo
4. Comet
5. Super-Turtle
6. Fuzzy
7. Ace
8. Robin Robin
9. Batcow
10. Jumpa
11. Whatzit
12. Hoppy
13. Storm
14. Topo
15. Ark
16. Fluffy
17. Proty
18. Gleek
19. Big Ted
20. Dawg
21. Paw Pooch
22. Bull Dog
23. Chameleon Collie
24. Hot Dog
25. Tail Terrier
26. Tusky Husky
27. Mammoth Mutt
28. Rex the Wonder Dog
29. B'dg
30. Sen-Tag
31. Fendor
32. Stripezoid
33. Zallion
34. Ribitz
35. Bzzd
36. Gratch
37. Buzzoo
38. Fossfur
39. Zhoomp
40. Eeny

 1

 2

 3

 4

 5

 6

 7

 8

 9

 10

 11

 12

 13

 14

 15

 16

 17

 18

 19

 20

 21

 22

 23

 24

 25

 26

 27

 28

 29

 30

 31

 32

 33

 34

 35

 36

 37

 38

 39

 40

KNOW YOUR VILLAIN PETS!

1. Bizarro Krypto
2. Ignatius
3. Brainicat
4. Mechanikat
5. Crackers
6. Giggles
7. Joker Fish
8. Rozz
9. Artie Puffin
10. Griff
11. Waddles
12. Mad Catter
13. Dogwood
14. Chauncey
15. Misty
16. Sneezers
17. General Manx
18. Nizz
19. Fer-El
20. Titano
21. Mr. Mind
22. Sobek
23. Bit-Bit
24. X-43
25. Starro
26. Dex-Starr
27. Glomulus
28. Rhinoldo
29. Whoosh
30. Pronto
31. Snorrt
32. Rolf
33. Squealer
34. Kajunn
35. Tootz
36. Eezix
37. Donald
38. Waxxee
39. Fimble
40. Webbik

MEET THE AUTHOR!

Donald Lemke

Donald Lemke works as a children's book editor. He has written dozens of comic books, including the Zinc Alloy series and the adventures of Bike Rider, and many chapter books for DC Comics. Donald lives in Minnesota with his beautiful wife, Amy, and their not-so-golden retriever, Paulie.

MEET THE ILLUSTRATOR!

Eisner Award-winner Art Baltazar

Art Baltazar is a cartoonist machine from the heart of Chicago! He defines cartoons and comics not only as an art style, but as a way of life. Currently, Art is the creative force behind *The New York Times* best-selling, Eisner Award-winning, DC Comics series Tiny Titans, and the co-writer for *Billy Batson and the Magic of SHAZAM!* Art is living the dream! He draws comics and never has to leave the house. He lives with his lovely wife, Rose, big boy Sonny, little boy Gordon, and little girl Audrey. Right on!

WORD POWER!

boot camp (BOOT KAMP)—a place for training new recruits

cadet (kuh-DET)—a young person who is training to become a member of a force

obstacle (OB-stuh-kuhl)—something that gets in your way or prevents you from doing something

puny (PYOO-nee)—small and weak, or unimportant

quivering (KWIV-ur-ing)—trembling or vibrating

serum (SEER-uhm)—a liquid used to prevent or cure a disease

shivering (SHIV-ur-ing)—shaking with cold or fear

whimper (WIM-pur)—to make weak, crying noises

AW YEAH!

DC SUPER-PETS!
The AMAZING
Mini-Mutts
by Donald Lemke
Illustrated by
Art Baltazar

DC SUPER-PETS!
ATTACK OF THE
INVISIBLE
CATS
by Scott
Sonneborn
Illustrated by
Art Baltazar

DC SUPER-PETS!
BACKWARD
BOWWOW
by Sarah Hines
Stephens
Illustrated by
Art Baltazar

DC SUPER-PETS!
BARNYARD
BRAINWASH
by John
Sazaklis
Illustrated by
Art Baltazar

DC SUPER-PETS!
BATTLE BUGS
OF
OUTER SPACE
by Jane B. Mason
Illustrated by
Art Baltazar

DC SUPER-PETS!
CANDY STORE
CAPER
by John Sazaklis
Illustrated by
Art Baltazar

DC SUPER-PETS!
THE FASTEST
PET ON
EARTH
by
J.E. Bright
Illustrated by
Art Baltazar

DC SUPER-PETS!
HEROES
OF THE
HIGH SEAS
by J.E. Bright
Illustrated by
Art Baltazar

DC SUPER-PETS!
THE
HOPPING
HERO
by John
Sazaklis
Illustrated by
Art Baltazar

Read all of these totally awesome DC SUPER-PETS stories today!

THE FUN DOESN'T STOP HERE!

Discover more:

- Videos & Contests!
- Games & Puzzles!
- Heroes & Villains!
- Authors & Illustrators!

@ www.capstonekids.com

Find cool websites and more books like this one at www.facthound.com Just type in Book I.D. 9781404864887 and you're ready to go!

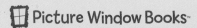

Picture Window Books™

Published in 2012
A Capstone Imprint
1710 Roe Crest Drive
North Mankato, MN 56003
www.capstonepub.com

STAR25290

Cataloging-in-Publication Data is available at the Library of Congress website.

ISBN: 978-1-4048-6488-7 (library binding)
ISBN: 978-1-4048-7218-9 (paperback)

Summary: Krypto, Ace, and other Super-Pet pooches visit the Bowwow Boot Camp to show a new breed of heroes a few old tricks. But the evil Brainicat wants to teach the canine cadets a lesson as well. When he shrinks them all to microscopic size, the prep-school pups must quickly learn to step up!

Art Director & Designer: Bob Lentz
Editor: Donald Lemke
Creative Director: Heather Kindseth
Editorial Director: Michael Dahl

Printed in the United States of America in Stevens Point, Wisconsin.
102011   006404WZS12

DC™
SUPER-PETS!

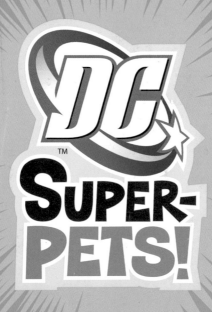

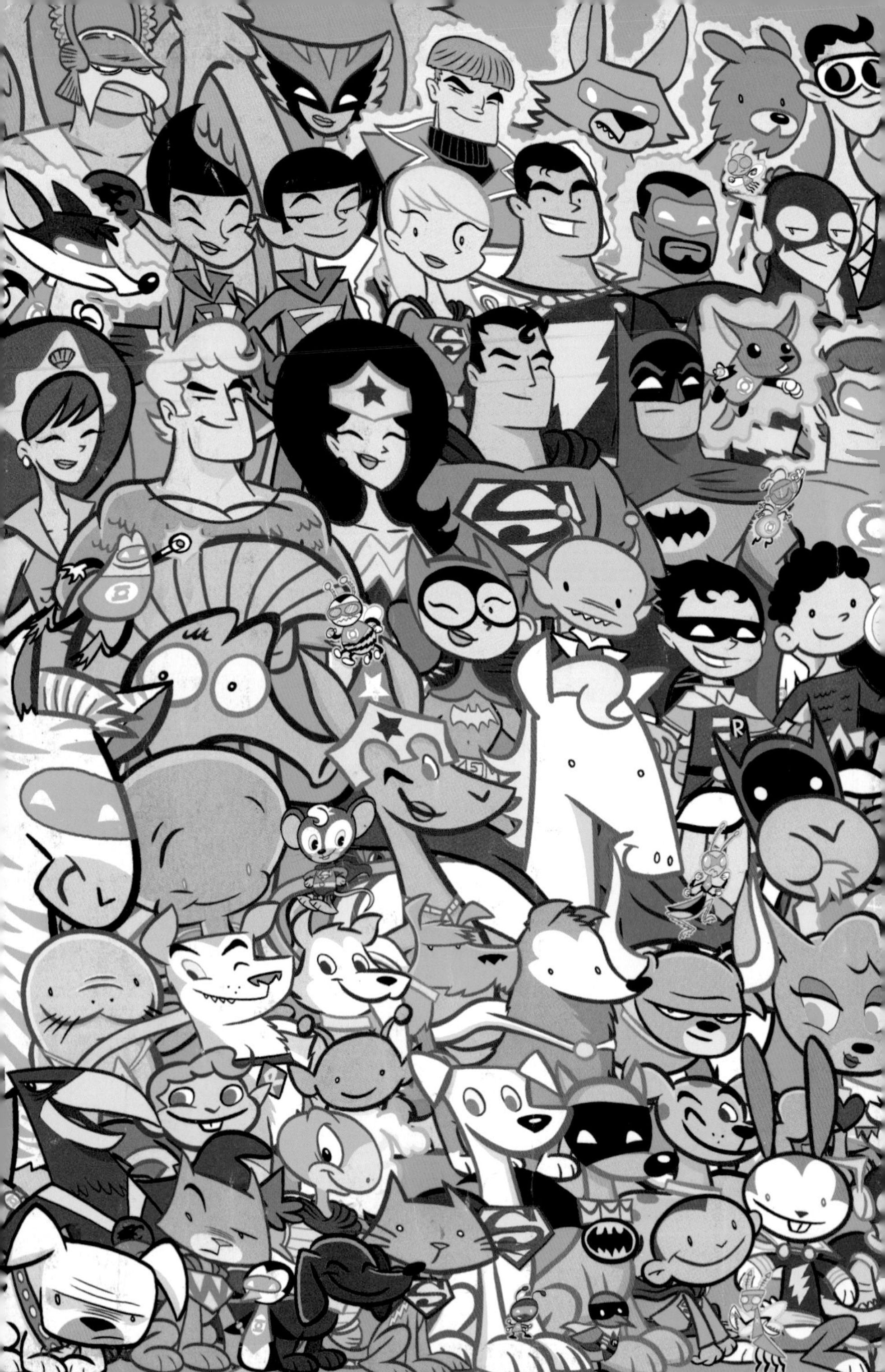